No Peacocks!

A Feathered Tale of Three Mischievous Foodies

Written by Robin Newman

Illustrated by Chris Ewald

Sky Pony Press

New York

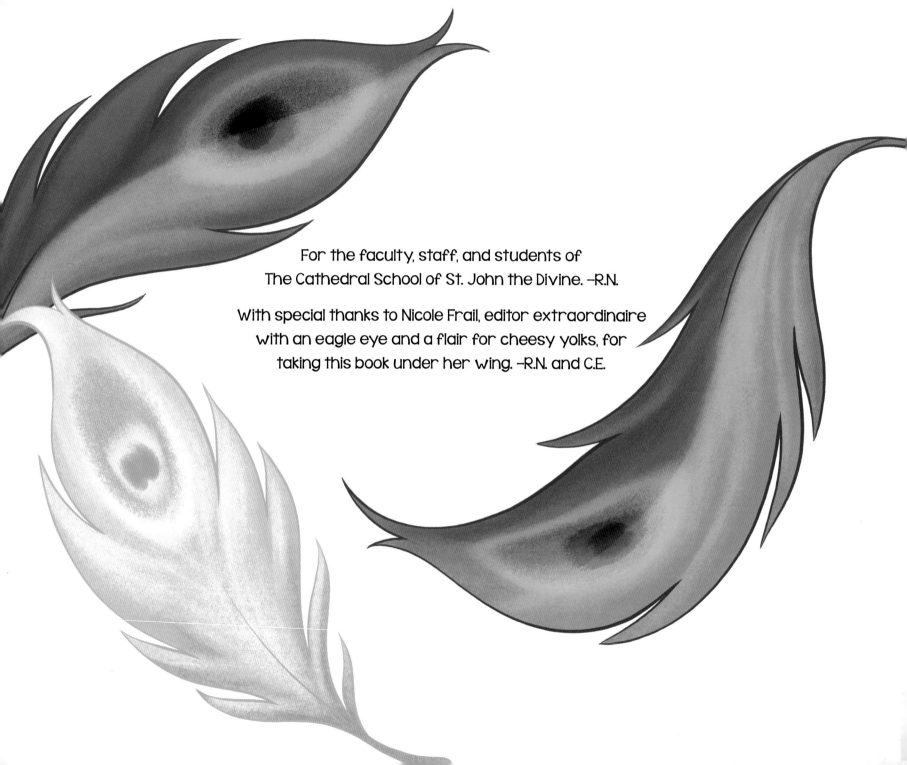

For the faculty, staff, and students of
The Cathedral School of St. John the Divine. –R.N.

With special thanks to Nicole Frail, editor extraordinaire
with an eagle eye and a flair for cheesy yolks, for
taking this book under her wing. –R.N. and C.E.

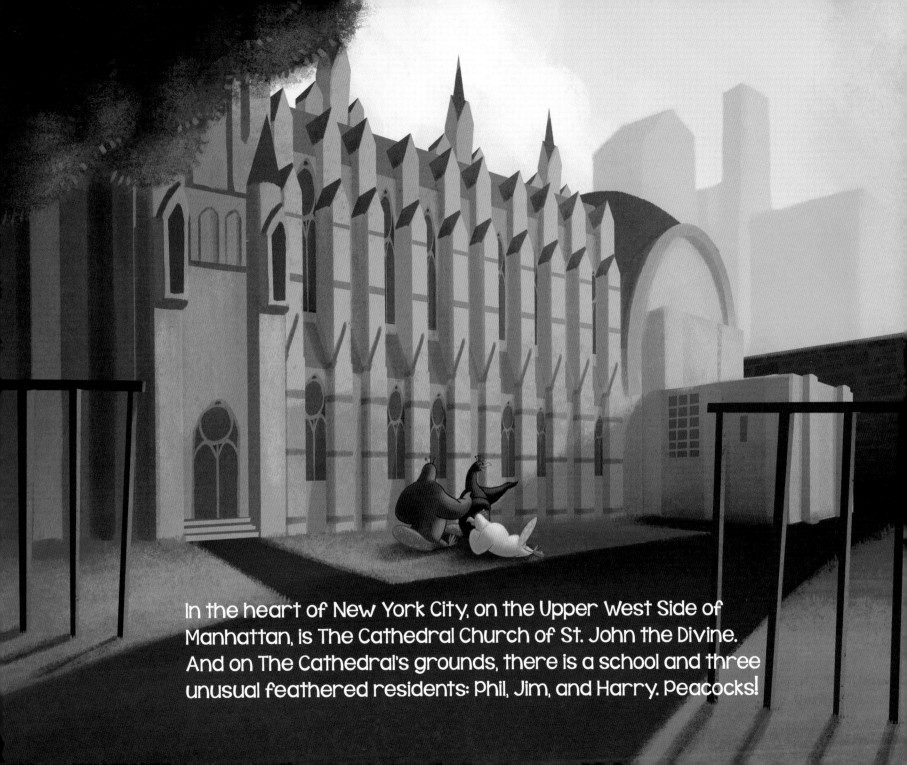

In the heart of New York City, on the Upper West Side of Manhattan, is The Cathedral Church of St. John the Divine. And on The Cathedral's grounds, there is a school and three unusual feathered residents: Phil, Jim, and Harry. Peacocks!

Every day the peacocks' caretaker feeds them sunflower seeds. Sunflower seeds for breakfast. Sunflower seeds for lunch. More for dinner.

"No peacocks!" cried the server at the pizzeria.

"No peacocks!" shouted the chef at the Chinese restaurant.

"No peacocks!" hollered
the baker at the pastry shop.

NO
PEACOCKS!

Everywhere
they went it was
the same story.

Each and every time they
were escorted back home.

"HOW," squawked Phil.
"INCREDIBLY," honked Jim.
"RUDE!" screeched Harry.

But then, they got a whiff of something yummy. They followed that
smell across the schoolyard, through the field, and past the garden.

It was coming from
the school's dining hall.

The students were eating ooey,
gooey, creamy and delicious
mac 'n cheese. The peacocks
had to try some.

Now, peacocks are not allowed in the
school. But this minor inconvenience
wasn't going to stop Phil, Jim, and Harry.

Every day, they lined up with the students.

Again and again they were told,
"No peacocks!"

They needed a plan.
They studied maps,
measured distances,
and calculated flight
trajectories . . .

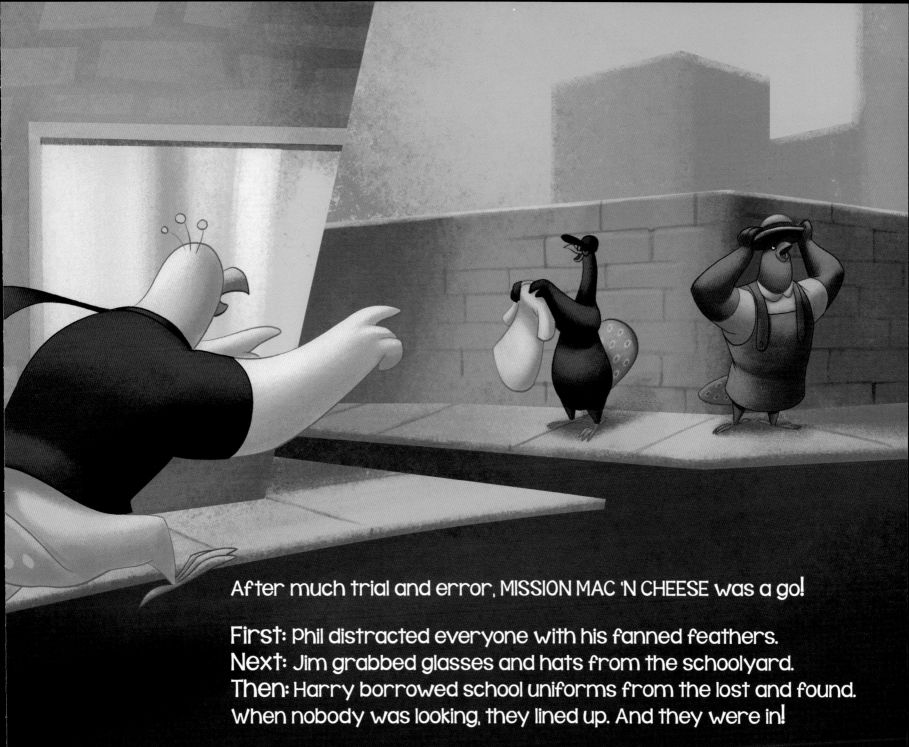

After much trial and error, MISSION MAC 'N CHEESE was a go!

First: Phil distracted everyone with his fanned feathers.
Next: Jim grabbed glasses and hats from the schoolyard.
Then: Harry borrowed school uniforms from the lost and found.
When nobody was looking, they lined up. And they were in!

But not where they wanted to be.
"Class, please take out your readers!" a teacher announced.

"Here," said a student, passing the birds a book.

They didn't know what to do.

"Like this," said another student. "Watch me!"

The birds tried their best to blend in but . . .

NOT . . .

ALWAYS . . .

SUCCESSFULLY!

The bell rang in the nick of time.

They rushed out of the classroom and made their way to the dining hall.

"Each of you take a tray," said a student. "Shhh! Be quiet!"

But Phil squawked with excitement.

Jim honked with joy.

Harry screeched with anticipation.

And Chef yelled, "PEACOCKS!"

They knew their goose was cooked. They were escorted back to their coop—without even a taste!

After school, they spotted a student in the schoolyard.

Phil waved her over.

Jim checked to make sure the coast was clear.

Harry handed her a picture of the mac 'n cheese.

The student looked around and nodded.
"I've got a connection. I'll take care of it, but it'll cost you three feathers. Meet me here when the bells ring. Make sure you're not followed."

The meeting went as planned.
The exchange was made.

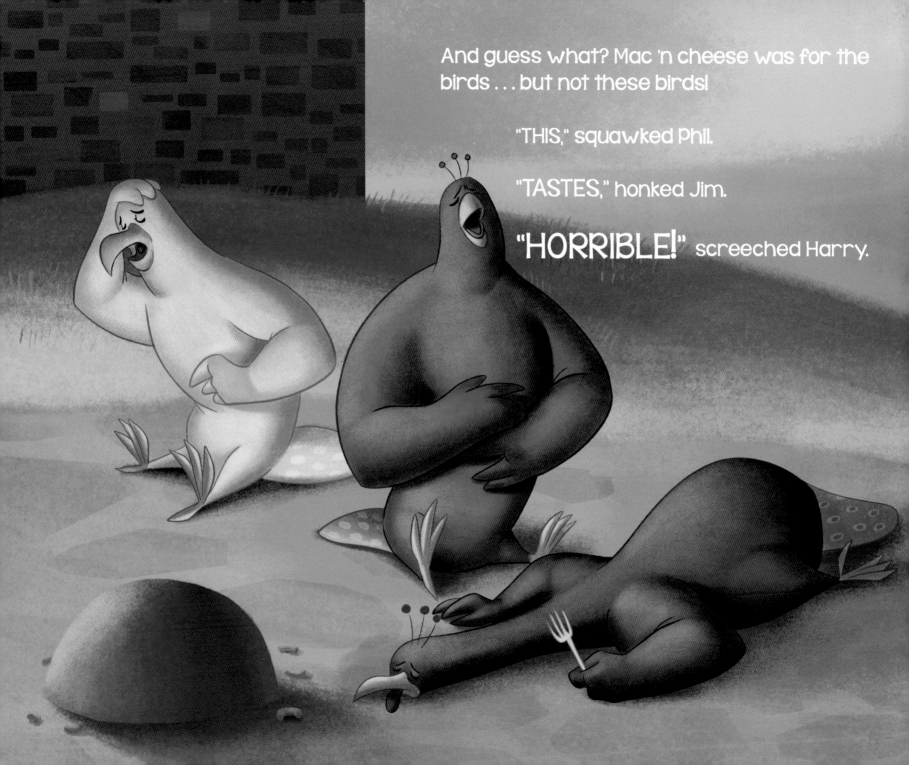

And guess what? Mac 'n cheese was for the birds . . . but not these birds!

"THIS," squawked Phil.

"TASTES," honked Jim.

"HORRIBLE!" screeched Harry.

Turns out sunflower seeds weren't so bad after all.

But from time to time,
the peacocks still like
trying something new.

On 112th Street and Amsterdam Avenue, you will find three beautifully plumaged neighborhood celebrities residing on the 11.3-acre grounds of The Cathedral Church of St. John the Divine.

Phil is a leucistic white peafowl, and Jim and Harry are your traditional blue and green peacocks.

Jim and Harry arrived at The Cathedral in 2002. Phil was a later addition. Jim is named for the dean of The Cathedral, The Very Reverend Dr. James A. Kowalski; Harry for a former dean, The Very Reverend Harry H. Pritchett Jr.; and Phil, for Phillip Foote, the former head of The Cathedral School.

The peacocks roam the grounds freely. When they were younger, they frequently wandered off the grounds. I've heard they've been caught near the Hungarian Pastry Shop across the street and have even ventured down to Broadway and Morningside Drive. On one occasion, Phil disappeared for four days and was found on 108th Street and Broadway. But everyone in the neighborhood knows the birds, and if they roam off the grounds, The Cathedral gets a call to come pick them up.

And the peacocks really are foodies! They eat anything and everything they find on the grounds. They're extremely fond of the tomato plants. They're fed protein-based pellets three times a day, and their diet is supplemented with grapes, peanuts, almonds, sunflower seeds, lettuce, and kelp.

They are not allowed to eat mac 'n cheese.

The children love the peacocks. When my son attended the school, every morning I would hear shouts of "peacock!" when one had been spotted. And you never knew when or where you were going to see one, two, or even all three of them. You could often find one on the school's porch at pick up or on top of the playground's jungle gym.

From the first moment I saw the dynamic feathered trio, I knew that I wanted to write a story about them. But it wasn't until I was attending a meeting at the school, and someone announced—"Did anyone leave a stroller on the porch with a sandwich? Because one of the peacocks just ate it."—that I knew the kind of story I wanted to write.

Speaking of food, the school's mac 'n cheese is the best in the world.

On Twitter, you can follow Phil: @CathedralPhil

Or, check him out on YouTube: http://www.youtube.com/CathedralPhil.

Resources

Alvarez, Maria. "Peacocks continue a tradition at St. John the Divine." *Newsday*. May 31, 2012. http://www.newsday.com/news/peacocks-continue-a-tradition-at-st-john-the-divine-1.3754326?firstfree=yes.

Barron, James. "On Godly Grounds, a Prideful Flock." *The New York Times City Room* Web. January 31, 2012. http://cityroom.blogs.nytimes.com/2012/01/31/for-jim-phil-and-harry-cathedral-grounds-are-home/.

Barron, James. "Construction Project at a Cathedral: A New Home for Its Peacocks." *The New York Times*. October 8, 2017. https://www.nytimes.com/2017/10/08/nyregion/peacocks-st-john-the-divine.html?smid=tw-share.

Chan, Sewell. "At a Peacock Sanctuary, Mourning a Slain Relative." *The New York Times City Room* Web. July 2, 2007. http://cityroom.blogs.nytimes.com/2007/07/02/at-a-peacock-sanctuary-mourning-a-slain-relative/comment-page-1/.

Crow, Kelly. "A Real City Bird: Cathedral's Peacock Is Treated for Malaise." *The New York Times Neighborhood Report: Morningside Heights* Web. February 10, 2002. http://www.nytimes.com/2002/02/10/nyregion/neighborhood-report-morningside-heights-real-city-bird-cathedral-s-peacock.html.

Petslady. "Cathedral Phil the Peacock Tweets from St. John the Divine." Web. August 22, 2012. http://en.paperblog.com/cathedral-phil-the-peacock-tweets-from-st-john-the-divine-nyc-290571/.

Plitt, Amy. "Animal Mascots of NYC." *Time Out New York*. July 19, 2011. http://www.timeout.com/newyork/shopping/animal-mascots-of-nyc-specialists?pageNumber=4.

Weil, Jennifer. "Peacock Earns Heavenly Nest." *New York Daily News*. March 21, 2002. http://www.nydailynews.com/archives/boroughs/peacock-earns-heavenly-nest-article-1.487968.

Copyright © 2018 by Robin Newman

Illustrations copyright © 2018 by Christopher Ewald

All rights reserved. No part of this book may be reproduced in any manner without the express written consent of the publisher, except in the case of brief excerpts in critical reviews or articles. All inquiries should be addressed to Sky Pony Press, 307 West 36th Street, 11th Floor, New York, NY 10018.

First Edition

This is a work of fiction. Names, characters, places, and incidents are from the author's imagination, and used fictitiously.

Sky Pony Press books may be purchased in bulk at special discounts for sales promotion, corporate gifts, fund-raising, or educational purposes. Special editions can also be created to specifications. For details, contact the Special Sales Department, Sky Pony Press, 307 West 36th Street, 11th Floor, New York, NY 10018 or info@skyhorsepublishing.com.

Sky Pony® is a registered trademark of Skyhorse Publishing, Inc.®, a Delaware corporation.

Visit our website at www.skyponypress.com.

10 9 8 7 6 5 4 3 2 1

Library of Congress Cataloging-in-Publication Data is available on file.

Cover design by Kate Gardner
Cover illustration by Christopher Ewald

Print ISBN: 978-1-5107-1480-9
Ebook ISBN: 978-1-5107-1481-6

Printed in China